copy gg³³

Martha

For my son Ilya.

Gennady Spirin

Martha

PHILOMEL BOOKS
NEW YORK

This all happened in Moscow when my family was young.

It was a snowy winter day outside. Inside, it was warm and cozy. My wife, Raya, and our five-year-old son, Ilya, had just returned from a walk. Ilya ran to me without taking off his outside clothes.

"Papa," he said, "I found a crow with a broken wing."

Raya walked in, holding something in her arms, wrapped in her beautiful wool shawl. I saw the small, black head of a crow, its eyes frightened, its mouth soundlessly open.

"We found it in the park, Papa," Ilya said. "It was dragging its wing along the snow." It had left a bloody trail. It hadn't even resisted when they picked it up.

Raya quickly took the crow to the sink. She washed out the crow's wounds and put on a salve. Then she bandaged the crow's whole body—it looked like a funny white doll with a black crow head and tail and two elegant feet.

Ilya was fascinated. He didn't utter a word. I wondered what we would do with this crow!

Raya put the crow in a big wicker basket right next to my drawing table. That day, the crow did not eat or utter a sound.

In the morning we took the crow to the veterinarian. The reception room was full of people and animals—cats and dogs of all kinds, two parrots, one beautiful-feathered rooster.

The veterinarian looked at the broken wing and shook his head. "Put it to sleep. A crow with a broken wing cannot live long in the wild. And if you keep it, you will have it a lifetime!"

"No," exclaimed Ilya. "The crow is going to get better and then fly."

"No, child," the doctor said. "This bird will never fly again." He looked at Raya and me. "Put it to sleep."

"Mama, Papa. I am not going to let him! This is my crow!" Ilya covered the basket with his hand.

And so this is the way the crow ended up living with us. Soon, we discovered the crow was not an it; the crow was a she, and we named her Martha.

Raya took care of her. She fed her in her arms. Martha began to accept everything, even medicine. Ilya was always close by, helping his mother.

The crow lived and slept in the basket by my drawing table.

The days went by. One morning, Ilya and I saw Martha pull her bandages off—one at a time—with her shiny beak. We started helping her, when Ilya said, "Papa, look!"

Her wing still drooped, but her wound had started to heal!

Martha loved water. Raya filled up a bowl of water and put it in the middle of the floor. Martha dipped her beak into the bowl and began to clean herself!

But to clean the wing was painful. We tried to tie up her drooping wing, but no, Martha ripped the tape off.

At first she had a lot of trouble getting out of the basket. The droopy wing was always in the way. But finally, she climbed out. After that, she would stand on the rim or the handle of the basket for hours, looking around, examining everything near her.

One time, Martha astounded me: She walked right across my table, pecking this object and that object. Then she walked right up my hand and began to examine me.

After a few days, Martha bravely started to climb my arm. She made her way all the way to my shoulder. She studied my left ear in great detail, and carefully parted my hair with her beak.

Soon, Martha jumped up onto my head! I tried not to stir or move. I didn't want to scare her. After looking around the room from this new viewpoint, she began to search for something in my hair.

At that moment, Ilya burst into the room, making a loud racket. Martha flew up onto the bookcase! She cawed loudly.

We started to laugh. Ilya ran out of the room to tell his mother. "Mama," he shouted, "Martha can fly."

Ilya had been right—Martha could fly.

Now she practiced tirelessly every day. She flew from the basket to my head, from my head to the bookcase, from the bookcase to a dresser, and then back to the basket. It was not so easy to draw with Martha using my head as her landing platform.

It was as if she understood the problem. She changed her route, instead landing on the head of a statue of Hermes that stood nearby.

And now I noticed that her wing wasn't droopy any longer. It was working perfectly.

From day to day she flew more and more confidently. The warm weather came. I opened my window, confident in Martha's good sense. Indeed, to my amazement, she would stroll across the window ledge without flying away.

She liked her new open space. She would observe the life on the street, and sometimes answer passing crows, *"Karrr!"*

Martha had gotten used to all of us. She still took food from Raya. She would travel along Ilya's outstretched arm up to his head. Ilya was happy with this. And she still felt at home on my table.

Martha was part of our family.

Then, one afternoon, we returned from a stroll and saw Martha on the windowsill. Her head was turned toward us, her black eyes twinkled, and her beak was half open. She pushed off from the windowsill and flew out.

"Martha!" Ilya called.

At first she seemed dragged down, but then she evened herself out, climbed higher into the air, and landed on the roof of a neighboring house. "Karrr," was her victorious call.

We ran into the house and up to her window. She flew by our window once, and then again, and then she disappeared from sight. We stood at the window waiting for Martha to come back, but she never did.

The summer passed. We came back from our *dacha*—that is a holiday cottage in the country—to Moscow. One morning, Ilya looked out of my window. "Martha!" he shouted. "Martha!"

Next to my window, on the branches of a tree, we saw a crow's nest. In it were nestlings and a mother crow. Was Martha this beautiful bird? I cannot say yes, I cannot say no, but Ilya firmly believed the bird he saw was Martha. Still a part of the family.

PATRICIA LEE GAUCH, EDITOR

Designed by Semadar Megged.   Text set in 15-point Goudy.
The art was done in watercolor on Arches watercolor paper.

Library of Congress Cataloging-in-Publication Data
Spirin, Gennadii.
Martha / Gennady Spirin.   p. cm.   Summary: The author relates how he and
his Moscow family rescued Martha, a crow with a broken wing, and how she
joined their household.   [1. Crows—Fiction. 2. Animal rescue—Fiction.
3. Moscow (Russia)—Fiction. 4. Russia—Fiction.] I. Title.   PZ7.S7569Mar 2005
[E]—dc22   2004006735
ISBN 0-399-23980-4
1 3 5 7 9 10 8 6 4 2
First Impression

GENNADY SPIRIN was born outside of Moscow and was a successful artist and illustrator there for many years. He came to the United States in 1991 on an invitation from Philomel and Dial Press. Since then he has illustrated many beautiful books for Philomel, among them *Philipok, Jack and the Beanstalk*, and *The Tale of the Firebird*.

Mr. Spirin has received many international awards for his illustrations, including four Gold Medals from the Society of Illustrators, four *New York Times* Best Illustrated Book of the Year awards, the Premio Grafico at the Bologna Childen's Book Fair, and the Golden Apple of the Bratislava International Biennale of children's book illustration.

Mr. Spirin lives in Princeton, New Jersey, with his wife and three sons.

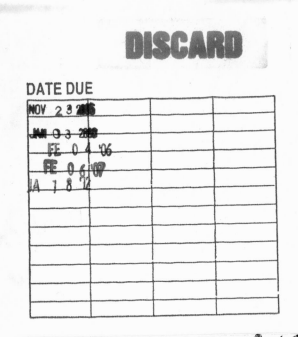